MO'S MISCHIEF

Best Friends

Titles in the Mo's Mischief series:

MO'S MISCHIEF

Best Friends

Hongying Yang

HarperTrophy®
An Imprint of HarperCollinsPublishers

Mo's Mischief: Best Friends
Text copyright © 2004 by Hongying Yang
English translation copyright © 2008 by HarperCollins Publishers
Illustrations copyright © 2003 by Pencil Tip Culture & Art Co.

Library of Congress catalog card number: 2008924435
ISBN 978-0-06-156476-5

◆

First published in China by Jieli Publishing House, 2004
First published in Great Britain by HarperCollins Children's Books, 2008
First U.S. Edition, 2008

BEST FRIENDS

Mo Shen Ma was the most mischievous child in Ms. Qin's class. With so many other students, Ms. Qin couldn't always keep an eye on Mo, so she asked Man Man to be Mo's desk-mate. Man Man enjoyed telling on Mo. She kept a little notebook, and any time Mo did something mischievous, she wrote it down for the teacher.

With Man Man watching him all the time, Mo couldn't get away with *anything*. So he was determined to sit next to someone else at school—and that someone was Lily.

Lily had perfect posture: she always kept her back straight and she always held her chin high. After all, she'd been going to ballet class since she was five years old!

Man Man and Lily were friends, but Man Man was a little jealous of Lily because she was so beautiful and graceful. So sometimes she would say something unkind about Lily behind her back.

One day Mo heard Man Man say that Lily was so full of herself that she didn't notice what anyone else was doing.

That gave Mo an idea! If Lily was his desk-mate instead of Man Man, she wouldn't notice any of his pranks because she was so full of herself! He would never get in trouble again.

Every day Mo imagined what it would be like to have Lily sit next to him. But how could he make it happen? Mo had another idea! He would ask his friends what they thought.

First he went and found Hippo.

"Guess who I want to sit next to, Hippo?"

Hippo didn't think about it, he just answered right away: "Monkey, of course. You talk to him all the time during class."

2

"Wrong. I don't want to be Monkey's desk-mate."

"Then it must be Penguin," said Hippo. "You want to eat the food he keeps in his desk."

Mo made a face. "Wrong again. Penguin's mean. He never wants to share anything, especially not his food. I definitely don't want to be his desk-mate."

Hippo grinned and turned red. "Do you want *me* to be your . . ."

Mo scowled. Hippo didn't have a clue. "Give up guessing, Hippo. I'll tell you. I want *Lily* to be my desk-mate."

"Oh . . . oh . . . I don't believe it!" exclaimed Hippo.

Mo was confused. "Why can't I have Lily as a desk-mate?"

"You just can't, that's why!" Hippo said.

Mo didn't know what he had said to make Hippo so upset. So he went to find Monkey and Penguin.

Mo found Monkey first and told him right away that he wanted to sit next to Lily.

Monkey laughed. "Really? You don't want to sit with Angel instead?"

Angel was Mo's neighbor. Mo thought she was kind of a pain because she was always hanging around

3

when he was with his friends.

"Is it because Lily's so pretty that you want to be her desk-mate?" asked Monkey.

"No, it's because Lily isn't interested in other people. So she won't notice when I get into mischief, and she won't tell on me to Ms. Qin," answered Mo.

Monkey snapped back, "Angel won't tattle on you either. Why don't you want to be *her* desk-mate?"

Huh, thought Mo. *What's the point of having friends if they won't help you when you need it the most?*

So Mo placed all his hopes on his *really* good friend Penguin, who *was* Lily's desk-mate. He hoped Penguin would change seats with him. He knew just how to get around Penguin!

Mo took a bag of potato chips from his backpack and went and found Penguin.

"Penguin, will you change places with me so that I can sit next to Lily?" asked Mo in his most friendly voice. He handed the bag of chips to Penguin. "Is that okay, Penguin?"

"It doesn't matter whether I say it's okay or not," Penguin said while cramming the chips into his mouth. "Ms. Qin isn't going to agree anyway."

Mo begged. "But if you told Ms. Qin that you'd like to sit next to someone else, you could let me sit next to Lily. . . ."

"No, I like sitting next to Lily," said Penguin, stuffing more chips into his mouth.

Mo was fed up. Here was another friend who wouldn't help him, and it had cost him a bag of potato chips. He shoved Penguin and Penguin shoved him back.

Unfortunately for both of them, two sixth graders saw everything and Mo and Penguin were sent to stand outside Ms. Qin's office.

It's not fair, thought Mo. *What's the point of best friends if they won't stick up for you?*

"It's not fair," said Penguin. "They'll take my chips away."

MS. QIN FINDS OUT

Ms. Qin frowned when she saw Mo and Penguin standing outside her office. "What have you two been up to now?" she asked.

They didn't want to tell Ms. Qin that they'd argued over Lily. The two boys stood there, looking down at the ground.

"Aren't you going to tell me? Okay, then you can stand here while I call your parents. They'll have to come and pick you up."

Penguin couldn't wait that long. He would miss his favorite cartoon if he had to wait for his dad to finish work.

"Okay, Ms. Qin, I'll tell you," Penguin spluttered.

Mo didn't expect Penguin to give him up so quickly. He glared at Penguin.

But Penguin thought the cartoon was more important than Mo, so he ignored him. "Mo wanted me to let Lily sit with him, and I refused. He shoved me and I shoved him back."

Ms. Qin was shocked. "Is that true, Mo?"

Now Mo may have been the most mischievous boy in her class, but Ms. Qin knew he always told the truth.

Mo admitted that what Penguin had said was true.

Ms. Qin said, "You may leave now, Penguin."

Penguin raced off. He could only think about getting home to his cartoon.

After he'd gone, Ms. Qin asked Mo to sit down. Then she said in a gentle voice, "Now Mo, why do you want to sit next to Lily?"

Mo was about to tell Ms. Qin that he wanted to sit next to Lily because he didn't want to sit next to Man Man anymore because she wrote down all his mischief in her notebook. But he stopped. He knew Man Man was Ms. Qin's favorite student, and that Ms. Qin had asked Man Man to keep an eye on Mo.

Mo said nothing and just looked down at the floor.

"Why won't you tell me, Mo? Is it because you *like* Lily?"

He nodded but then shook his head.

"What do you mean by that? Do you like her or not?" asked Ms. Qin.

"Sometimes I do, and sometimes I don't," Mo replied.

"Come on, Mo," Ms. Qin said. "When do you like her? And when don't you like her?"

"If she talks to me, I like her. If she doesn't, I don't."

"So . . . do you want her to notice you?"

Mo nodded.

Ms. Qin frowned. "You shouldn't be thinking about Lily so much, Mo. You should be concentrating on your schoolwork," she said.

"But it's natural for a boy to like a girl, isn't it, Ms. Qin?" Mo asked boldly.

"Not at such a young age, Mo!"

"At what age *can* I like her then, Ms. Qin?" asked Mo.

Ms. Qin knew that Mo didn't mean to make her upset, he was just being mischievous.

"Mo, stop being silly. I'm not wasting any more time with you. Lily will continue sitting next to Penguin and you must start behaving."

Then she took out a piece of paper from the drawer and began to write. When she finished, she folded the paper and put it into an envelope, but she didn't seal it.

She handed the envelope to Mo and said, "Give this to your father for me. Can I trust you to do that, Mo?"

"Of course, Ms. Qin." Mo remembered the time that Ms. Qin had told him she trusted him, and he felt a warm glow. He liked doing things for his teacher, but she didn't ask him often. Ms. Qin always asked teacher's pet Man Man or slimy Wen to help her. Mo knew he would never be the teacher's pet—there was no chance of that at all.

Mo took the letter and hurried home.

A DECORATED LETTER

Mo was longing to see what Ms. Qin had written in the letter. He knew the envelope wasn't sealed so he could easily sneak a look. But he knew it was wrong to read something that was meant for someone else. So Mo decided to glue the envelope shut so he wouldn't be tempted to open it. Then he decided to decorate the envelope by sticking feathers on it. This would make it look really important, as if a bird had delivered it urgently!

Mo went onto the balcony of his apartment, but no passing birds had dropped any feathers there.

He looked around his apartment to see what else he could use, and in a vase there was a beautiful peacock's feather that his mother had found on vacation once.

The feather was a bit too long, so Mo cut out the most beautiful eye parts of the feather to stick onto the envelope—three bright blue eyes to attract attention.

Mo placed the letter inside the display case in the hall, just below his father's gold trophy, the one he'd won for his toy designs. It was Mr. Ma's proudest possession—one he looked at every day when he came home from work.

When Mr. Ma came home, he looked at the gold trophy in the display case. Then he noticed the letter with the peacock-feather eyes.

"What's this, Mo?" he asked.

"Ms. Qin wrote you a letter," Mo answered. "It's quite important! It flew here! That's why it has a feather on it."

Mr. Ma didn't open the letter but held it high and asked jokingly, "Did Ms. Qin decorate the envelope, or did you? It looks suspiciously like your mother's favorite peacock feather—we will have to get her another one."

Mo confessed.

Then Mo's dad asked what the letter said.

"How should I know?" Mo replied. "The letter's to you, not me."

Mr. Ma opened the letter and began to read it carefully. He looked very serious. Mo was getting worried. . . .

"Mo, come here. I must have a talk with you, man to man."

Mo knew all about his dad's man-to-man talks. They'd had plenty in the past. It was usually when they talked about Mo's mother, Honeybunch.

But this time, Mr. Ma wasn't prepared for the talk. He read Ms. Qin's letter again from the very beginning, and then said, "Mo, Ms. Qin is worried that your feelings for a girl are getting in the way of your schoolwork."

Mo was astounded. What had begun as a simple idea for changing seats at school was turning into something very complicated. "What?" he asked.

"It seems there's something going on with a girl named Lily," said Mr. Ma.

"No! Lily doesn't even notice me."

"Then if she doesn't notice you, why do you like her?" Mr. Ma asked. "That doesn't make sense."

"Lily *sometimes* notices me," Mo said. "I just want to sit with her instead of Man Man."

"Is it because you think Lily is beautiful, and Man Man is not?"

"Dad . . ." Mo groaned.

"From what I remember of Man Man, she has a

nice smile," said Mr. Ma.

"But she never smiles at me. She's always telling on me to Ms. Qin," Mo said angrily.

"Does Lily smile at you?"

"No, but she doesn't smile at anyone, only at herself in the mirror," said Mo. "The only girl in the class who smiles at me is Angel."

"So why not sit with Angel?"

"Dad . . ." Mo yelled, getting really flustered.

Mr. Ma had other things to do. He needed to put a stop to this conversation. "Mo, I want you to write a letter to Ms. Qin saying that you will stop having these silly thoughts about Lily and start concentrating on your schoolwork."

"But Dad, is it *wrong* to like Lily?"

"Not wrong, but . . ."

Mo looked at his father expectantly.

"But . . ." Mr. Ma stammered. "You are too young to be taking girls quite so seriously."

"Am I too young to like someone?" Mo asked quickly. "Does that mean I'm too young to like you and Mom?" He just didn't get it.

"That's quite different, Mo, and you know it," said Mr. Ma. "Stop being so silly."

But Mo wouldn't let it rest. "But just WHAT is different about it, Dad?"

Mo's father had nothing to say. He knew Mo was right—he was only a kid. Mo didn't have complicated feelings like adults did—he either liked someone or he didn't. What was the harm in that? He told Mo not to bother writing to Ms. Qin. He would go and see her himself.

LiLY CHANGES SEATS

Mr. Ma stood quietly before Ms. Qin. She was so strict, he felt like a schoolboy again!

This wasn't the first time Mr. Ma had been to see Ms. Qin. That was the problem when your son was one of the most mischievous boys in the school.

"Have you spoken to your son about his feelings for Lily?" asked Ms. Qin.

"Yes, I have," replied Mo's dad.

"Does he realize the foolishness of his puppy love?"

"It's not so serious, is it?" he replied.

"Not so serious?" She raised her voice and said

angrily, "Your son is far too young to have those sorts of feelings for a girl."

"Calm down, Ms. Qin," said Mr. Ma. "I used to think I loved a girl when I was Mo's age. The next day she wouldn't let me be on her team so I stopped loving her right away! It's all part of growing up."

Hmph. Like father, like son, thought Ms. Qin. She was disappointed in Mr. Ma. She would have to sort the whole thing out herself.

After Mr. Ma left, Ms. Qin made a plan.

The first step was to put as much distance between Lily and Mo as she could.

Lily's seat was right behind Mo's. So she would have to move Lily to sit with Wen, whose desk was on the other side of the classroom.

The next day, Ms. Qin made the change.

"Why have you moved Lily away from Penguin, Ms. Qin?" Mo asked, puzzled.

Ms. Qin didn't answer him. *What a hopeless boy*, she thought. *He doesn't get it!*

Mo was fed up. He couldn't understand why Ms. Qin had moved Lily to sit next to Wen. He thought there must have been a problem with Penguin. Mo felt sorry for Penguin. Neither of them liked Wen—he was such a know-it-all, always using big words.

Penguin was fed up too. He liked sitting with Lily. He could get away with eating in class, because Lily didn't pay any attention to him. Penguin was a crybaby, so he started to cry.

"What's the matter, Penguin?" asked Ms. Qin.

Monkey raised his hand to speak. "Ms. Qin, Ms. Qin . . . please, please, I know why he's crying. He's upset because Lily isn't going to sit with him anymore."

"Thank you, Monkey, I can see that for myself!" Ms. Qin sighed.

Lily didn't pay attention to what was going on with her classmates. She wasn't really interested and thought it was none of her business. She collected her books, put them into her backpack, and went to her new seat without complaining.

Mo was confused: why did Ms. Qin move Lily away from Penguin when they were both so happy sitting together?

On the way home from school, Monkey asked Penguin why Ms. Qin had changed Lily's seat.

"How would I know? I have no idea what she thinks," Penguin said, sniffling.

"Well, I know why," Monkey said in a mysterious voice. "It's because of Mo."

"Mo?" said Penguin, blinking.

"You know, Mo wanted to sit next to Lily because he *loves* her, so Ms. Qin had to separate them."

Penguin was furious.

When Mo caught up with them, Penguin pushed him.

Not knowing why and not bothering to find out, Mo pushed him back.

Some of the other boys caught up with them. One of them was Wen.

When they saw Wen, Mo and Penguin stopped shoving each other and shouted at him instead. "What do you think you're looking at?"

"I can look, can't I? There's no law against it," said Wen.

"No. But you still can't do it," said Mo.

"Fine! Don't expect any help from me when you want to know a word for something."

Wen stormed off.

Monkey turned to Mo. "Who would you prefer Lily sat with—Penguin or Wen?"

Mo knew he would rather Lily sat with Penguin

than with Wen, who talked as if he had swallowed a dictionary. After all, Mo and Penguin were the best of friends, even if they did have a few playground fights. "Penguin," he said at last. He couldn't bear the idea of Lily being Wen's desk-mate forever!

"In that case," said Monkey, "I think I have a plan. . . ."

OPPOSITES

Monkey's plan was that Mo would tell Ms. Qin that he'd been silly and would now concentrate on his schoolwork and not on his feelings for Lily. Then he would ask her to move Lily back to sit with Penguin.

Mo didn't really want to do it, but he gave in because Penguin was his friend. He wrote a letter to Ms. Qin. He wrote, *I promise to hate Lily*.

The next day, Mo gave the letter to Ms. Qin.

"Ms. Qin, it's all my fault," he declared, passing the letter to her. "This is my guarantee that there will be no more silliness from me."

Ms. Qin was astonished. Mo had written something without her asking him to!

She was even more astonished when she read the letter.

"Why are you promising to *hate* Lily?" she asked Mo.

"Because 'hate' is the opposite of 'like' and you wanted me to stop liking Lily and start doing my schoolwork."

"That's not quite right, Mo," said Ms. Qin. "You shouldn't hate *any* of your classmates."

"But if I can't *like* and I can't *hate*, what can I do?" said Mo.

"You can concentrate on your schoolwork," Ms. Qin replied.

"I will, if you will agree to move Lily back to sit with Penguin. Please, Ms. Qin?"

Ms. Qin was exasperated.

"That's enough, Mo!" she said firmly, and ordered him into class.

Penguin and Monkey asked him how the plan was going.

Mo shook his head.

He, too, was exasperated.

After school, Mo had a BIG surprise. Lily was waiting to talk to him.

"Why do you hate me, Mo?" she asked quietly.

Mo stared. "I don't hate you!"

"You *do* hate me," Lily said firmly. "You wrote to Ms. Qin, promising to hate me."

"How did you know that? Who told you?" asked Mo.

Mo *knew* it must have been Monkey. Monkey was such a gossip, he could *never* keep a secret.

"Tell me why, Mo!" Lily didn't know anyone who hated her. She'd grown up like a lovely princess—everybody loved her and she had gotten used to it. She was surprised, and a little shocked, to learn that Mo hated her. Lily had to find out why.

"Why? Tell me why?"

Mo was beginning to feel quite good. Lily didn't normally talk to him. But now she wouldn't leave him alone!

He began to walk home, ignoring her question. As a matter of fact, he couldn't tell her why he hated her, because he didn't hate her!

The more Mo ignored Lily, the more she wanted his attention. She started to compliment him.

"You look so cool, Mo! I love those shoes you're wearing."

He was so happy he nearly jumped for joy. No girl had ever praised him like that except Angel, and she didn't count. And Lily was the most beautiful girl in the school.

Lily kept following him until they got to his house. Mo would have invited Lily over and offered her some ice cream. But he was beginning to learn how to be cool. If he gave in now, Lily might never notice him again.

Mo said to her rather rudely, "Well, that's it. I'm home. Good-bye."

"Please, Mo, please tell me!" Lily was desperate for an answer.

Mo was so happy, but he wasn't going to show it.

"I won't tell you. Ever!" yelled Mo. "Go home. Your mother will be wondering where her little ballerina is." He was shaking inside because he HATED being so mean to someone else. Perhaps being cool wasn't such a good thing.

Lily left.

Mo watched her go and felt like crying. He wondered whether Lily felt the same.

He was sorry he hadn't invited her inside. But he decided that if ignoring Lily made her notice him, then so be it. That was the way things would be.

Mo's day had suddenly gotten much brighter!

PHOTO SHOOT

It was nearly Children's Day and the school was holding a big celebration in the auditorium. Every class was performing and Lily had been chosen from Mo's class to perform her *Swan Lake* ballet role.

Whenever she performed, Lily asked people to take photos for her. She had a packed photo album full of her dance photos.

Lily wanted Hippo to take photos for her on Children's Day because he was quiet and serious and not noisy or mischievous like some of the other boys. Hippo never said much. And he was the tallest boy in class. Lily thought he was really cool!

Lily raised her chin and walked in ballet steps to Hippo where he was playing Ping-Pong with Mo, Monkey, and Penguin.

"Hippo, can you use a camera?" Lily asked directly, since a beautiful girl doesn't need to beat around the bush. "Will you take photos of my dance performance tomorrow, please?"

Before Hippo had even opened his mouth, Mo and Monkey started teasing.

"Hippo won't be able to keep his mind on the photos."

"His hand will be shaking too much to press the button."

"I . . . I . . ."

Hippo couldn't get a word in edgewise.

Mo announced, "My dad bought a fantastic camera in Japan. All the celebrity photographers use one like it. Lily, I'll take great photos of you with it."

Penguin pushed Mo aside and said, "Lily, I can bring my video camera and you can have a video of your complete performance, with music too."

The boys were talking so excitedly that Wen overheard their conversation. He had an idea. . . .

 29

After school Mo got home and rushed into the apartment.

"Dad, Dad, Lily's going to perform ballet in school tomorrow for Children's Day. Can I take your special camera to school so I can take pictures of her? PLEASE?"

Mr. Ma didn't really want Mo to take the camera to school, but Mo was his only, very special son, and Mr. Ma could never quite say no to him. Mo rushed to get the camera.

"Dad, Dad, has the camera got film in it?" Mo demanded.

Mr. Ma used the camera a lot for his work and he always had lots of film that he kept in the refrigerator. He took out a roll of film and was just about to put it in the camera when Mo shouted again. "Dad, Dad, can I use the tripod?"

"You won't need a tripod, Mo," said Mr. Ma, still holding the film in his hand.

"But I will," said Mo. "My hands might shake when I take the pictures for Lily. Then they'll come out all blurry."

So Mr. Ma—very reluctantly—showed Mo how to use the tripod and the camera.

The next day, Mo went to school with the camera hanging around his neck and the tripod slung over his shoulder.

"Mo, what on earth are you carrying all that equipment for?" Ms. Qin asked. She thought that Mo was up to mischief again.

"I'm going to take photos of Lily's ballet performance."

"Did you get permission from me or from Lily?" asked Ms. Qin.

"Lily said I could. If you don't believe me, ask Penguin. He was there when she said it."

Penguin had his video camera with him. Before Ms. Qin had a chance to ask him, he said, "Lily said she would dance much better if someone was taking photos of her. She said she might not dance as well if no one was taking photos."

Ms. Qin sighed. There was only one Children's Day a year, she supposed. "Fine," she agreed. "But don't distract Lily when she's dancing."

Mo felt very important. He was showing off a little bit, with the camera hanging around his neck and the tripod resting on his shoulder. But his bubble was about to be burst by Wen, who had a plan of his own. . . .

Wen walked up to Mo and watched him for a while. Then he said, "Gee, Mo, you've got a huge camera!"

"It will be even bigger when I use the zoom lens!" Mo laughed.

Mo held the camera and pressed a button. An enormous lens zoomed out in less than a second.

"Wow!" said all the kids standing around.

"See?" Mo said to Wen. "This is a *professional* camera!"

Wen smiled slyly and walked away.

The celebration began. The principal's speech was followed by performances by each class. Lily's dance was last . . . and the best one, thought Mo. Mo hadn't paid much attention to the other performances—he was too busy fiddling with his camera and tripod. But when Lily came on stage, he was ready for action.

Mo rushed onto the stage to be closer to Lily.

"Mo, what on earth are you doing?" asked Ms. Qin, pulling him back. "Get down! Get down quickly!"

"I need to be on stage to take good photos of Lily!"

"Photos must be taken OFF the stage, not on it. The stage is only for performers!"

Now Mo was flustered. When he assembled the tripod, he pulled out the legs, but they weren't the right height. But when the tripod was high enough, the legs closed in again. Then Mo couldn't screw the camera into the tripod. He had already missed shooting the beginning of Lily's ballet. Never mind, there was plenty more to come.

But there were lots of flashes going off. Mo couldn't understand who else was taking photos of Lily.

Then he saw the photographer—it was Wen. He was holding a tiny camera, taking photos very, very quickly. He didn't have a tripod. He didn't have a zoom lens . . . but he was definitely taking pictures of Lily!

Mo was not going to be outdone by Wen. He stopped fiddling with the tripod and laid it down on the floor. He held his camera and ran around as near to the stage as he could get, with the lens focused on Lily the whole time.

Click click click, Mo was taking photos nonstop.

When the performance was over, Wen bragged that he had taken more than one hundred photos of Lily.

Mo said he had taken more than *two* hundred photos of Lily. And since his large camera was much more sophisticated than Wen's tiny one, he knew he would have lots of good photos.

"But Mo, I didn't see you change your film once," said Wen, smiling. "What sort of film takes more than two hundred photos?"

Mo felt nauseated. He knew that rolls of film usually had twenty-four or thirty-six photos. But his dad had said this was a super-advanced camera from Japan, so maybe it would be okay.

"Wen, how can *you* be so sure that *your* camera has taken more than a hundred photos?" Mo asked.

"Let me tell you, Mo. Mine is a *digital* camera. It doesn't need film. More than four hundred pictures can be taken by just inserting a card in the camera. Is your brain big enough to understand that?"

Mo felt miserable.

"I bet your camera doesn't even have film in it," Wen said, pointing to the camera hanging around Mo's neck. "You'd better open it and see."

Now Mo had another problem. If he opened the camera and there *was* film in it, the light would ruin the photos. If he opened it and there *wasn't* film in it, his reputation would be ruined. It was a no-win situation.

"I DARE you to open it!" yelled Wen.

Wen was really getting on Mo's nerves. . . .

"OPEN, OPEN, OPEN!" everyone else chanted.

Mo's heart was pounding really fast. His hands were shaking. He opened the camera and . . .

There was NO film inside.

Mo had made a fool of himself and nothing anyone could say would make him feel better . . . yet.

Lily walked toward Mo wearing her snow-white dress and ballet shoes.

"How many photos did you take, Mo?"

"Over two hundred," said Wen before Mo could answer. "But he didn't have any film in his camera!"

"You are so mean, Mo!" she said. "I would have paid you for the film you used."

"I am not mean. I . . ." Mo was almost in tears.

"Lily, please come here!" a sly voice called out. Wen motioned to her mysteriously.

She went over and Wen handed her his digital camera. Lily looked at it and smiled.

Mo was so curious that he went over too. There was a little screen on the back of the camera, and Wen was showing Lily the photos one by one.

"But my eyes are shut in this one," exclaimed Lily. "And my mouth is open in this one."

"Never mind, we can delete those." Wen smirked.

"Wow! What a fantastic camera!"

Lily was so happy seeing Wen's photos, she had forgotten all about Mo's disaster. And Mo was so happy to see Lily happy that he forgot about it too.

That was the good thing about Mo Shen Ma: he never stayed upset for long because there were too many exciting things to do!

JEALOUSY

Every afternoon for the last few weeks, Angel's mother had been picking her up after school, getting into a taxi, and driving off in the opposite direction of their house.

"Lily, do you know where Angel goes with her mother after school?" asked Man Man. She liked to know EVERYTHING.

Lily said, "I haven't noticed her going anywhere. I'm not interested in what Angel does."

Lily never really noticed other people. She was much too interested in herself and she certainly wouldn't pay attention to someone shy like Angel.

"Something must have happened to Angel," Man Man said. "You could ask Mo about it."

"Why do you think Mo would know?" said Lily in a rather bored voice.

"Mo and Angel are neighbors. They usually know what each other's families are doing."

"Why don't you ask Mo yourself?" said Lily.

"You know we're not friends. If I asked him, he wouldn't tell me anything."

What Man Man said was true. If she asked Mo about it, he would definitely not say anything.

Mo was walking behind the girls with Hippo, Monkey, and Penguin. As usual they were being noisy and boisterous.

Lily turned back and moved toward them, holding her chin up high and gliding like a ballerina.

"Mo!"

Mo was excited when he heard Lily calling him. She usually liked to talk to Hippo, who was the coolest and tallest boy in class. Once Lily had been really impressed when Hippo tossed hard-boiled eggs into his mouth and ate them.

"Mo, where does Angel go with her mother after school?"

"Oh, they go to a TV studio—Angel is acting on a TV show," he said casually.

Everyone was AMAZED.

Monkey shouted first. "Mo, you must have made a mistake."

"Yeah!" said Penguin. "If you told me that Lily was on a TV show, I'd believe it. But Angel—she's such a mouse!" He laughed, then turned to Hippo. "Do you believe it?"

"No," said Hippo.

"Okay," said Mo. "Don't believe me if you don't want to."

Mo left them behind and walked off on his own.

"Mo!" said Lily, catching up with him quickly. "Is it really true that Angel is on a TV show?"

"Yes, it is. Why wouldn't it be true?" replied Mo.

Lily felt uncomfortable although she didn't know why she was so upset.

Man Man came up to her and asked, "Lily, what did Mo say?"

"I don't know! I don't know!"

Lily couldn't help crying. Afraid that Man Man would see her tears, she went home.

When she got home, Lily went to her bedroom and cried. She'd been learning ballet for years! Why couldn't *she* be on TV?

And how could someone as plain and boring as Angel be on a TV show?

Lily cried for a long time . . . and that's when she started to dislike Angel.

At school the next day, Angel had no idea that anything had happened. She smiled at Lily in her usual friendly way.

"Don't smile at me!" shouted Lily.

Lily banged the desk with her fist. This wasn't Lily the graceful ballet dancer, the beautiful swan who turns into a princess. This was an entirely different Lily.

Angel couldn't understand what was happening. She was scared to see Lily so angry.

"Lily, what's wrong with you?" she asked.

"Go away! Leave me alone!" yelled Lily.

In math class, Angel couldn't concentrate on her work. She kept wondering what she had done to upset

Lily. When the math teacher asked her the answer to a problem they'd been discussing, Angel just sat there in a trance.

"Angel, do you have any idea what the answer is?" The math teacher was annoyed with Angel and so were the other kids.

"I guess her mind is on other things, like starring on a TV show," a voice cried out.

It was Lily. The other students looked at her with

surprise, because she never called out in class.

"Lily, what did you say about starring on a TV show?"

Lily already regretted opening her mouth and she certainly wasn't going to say anything else.

So the math teacher asked Angel, "Is this true? Are you on a TV show, Angel?"

Angel nodded.

Then all the kids began whispering to one another. They were amazed. Angel was the last person they would have thought of as a celebrity.

After class, the math teacher took Angel to the office to see Ms. Qin.

Ms. Qin didn't believe Angel. She thought she was making it up.

"Angel, why are you pretending to be on a TV show?"

"It's true, Ms. Qin. My mother takes me to the TV studio every day after school."

"Well, Angel, I'm very surprised. I thought it would be Lily who went to the TV studios since she is already a performer *and* good at math. You should be concentrating on your schoolwork after school instead."

Lily saw Angel crying when she walked out of Ms. Qin's office. Lily didn't know what to think. She had been jealous because Angel was on a TV show and she wasn't, but she didn't like to see Angel cry.

THE TV DIRECTOR SPEAKS UP

Ms. Qin did not approve of Angel being on television when she couldn't do well on her schoolwork. So she asked Angel's mother to tell the director of the show that Angel had to stop going to the TV studio.

The television director had a loud, deep voice.

"But Angel is my star! She is one of the best actresses on the show," the director protested.

Angel hadn't known this before. She didn't know what to say.

The director spoke much louder, this time to Angel. "The show will be finished soon, so why can't you come anymore?"

Angel didn't want to admit that she didn't do well in school. Everyone on the show, from the director to the set designer and the lighting engineer to the camera operators, liked Angel very much because she was so good at acting. Unlike others on the cast, Angel could do her scenes in one shot, and she never forgot her lines. So Angel really didn't want them to know that she wasn't very good at school because they might think less of her. Angel said, "One girl in our class is very graceful and good at ballet, so perhaps she could be on the show instead of me?"

Angel meant Lily, of course. She knew that Lily was still angry with her. If she gave her role to Lily, maybe Lily wouldn't be angry anymore.

"Angel, don't be ridiculous! I want an actress, not a ballerina! Nobody is as good at acting as you."

"Lily could do better than me!" said Angel, on the verge of tears. "It's true. Director, please let her try out!"

"I don't want to have her try out." The director was

getting angry. "Angel, you have a contract. You have to finish filming."

So Angel had to tell the truth.

"Director, my teacher said I can't come to the TV studio anymore because it's affecting my grades at school." She sniffed.

The director looked at Angel and said gently, "All right, Angel, there's no need to get upset. I will go and talk to your teacher."

The next afternoon, the director went to the school to see Ms. Qin.

From the classroom window, Angel saw the director's car stop outside the school gate. She grabbed Lily's hand and ran downstairs.

"Leave me alone," yelled Lily. But she wasn't as strong as Angel and couldn't get away.

"Angel, stop it. What are you doing?"

"Got to see the director. The director is coming!" she panted.

They ran into the director at the bottom of the staircase.

"Director, director, this is Lily!" Angel pushed Lily forward. "Isn't she graceful? She can do ballet. . . ."

The director interrupted and said, "Angel, I have

come to see your teacher, not your friend!"

When Ms. Qin saw the director she was surprised.

The director got right to the point.

"Ms. Qin, I hear that you don't approve of Angel acting."

"That's correct," Ms. Qin said stiffly. "Angel cannot concentrate on her schoolwork. . . ."

How could Ms. Qin say such a thing to the director? Lily saw that Angel's face was quite red, and her eyes were filling with tears. She felt sorry for Angel.

When he saw her face, the director felt sorry for Angel too.

"Ms. Qin, Angel is an intelligent actress. She understands the script and acts so well and naturally. Please support her!"

Ms. Qin said, "Angel may be an intelligent actress, but she is not as intelligent with her schoolwork. She should be studying, not acting. I would prefer it if you used one of my *more* intelligent students."

Then she pointed at Lily. "Director, here is a more suitable child. Lily began to dance when she was five years old, and ballet has given her plenty of acting experience. Most importantly, she is very clever . . ."

The director could see that he was not going to get his own way with this teacher,

so he thought he'd better watch Lily dance.

Lily began to dance. Even without ballet shoes, she danced gracefully.

Ms. Qin was enchanted. Angel was enchanted. Even the director could see that Lily had talent . . .

. . . *ballet* talent.

After dancing, Lily waited for the director's decision.

The director said, "Lily, you dance very well and you hold yourself well. You are a natural ballerina, but you are not suitable to be an actress on my show. However, if you continue to dance, I am sure you will become a world-famous ballerina!"

Lily was so happy. Now someone had told her that she could be a world-famous ballerina and that's exactly what she wanted to be.

"Thank you, director!" Lily bowed to the director and then said to Ms. Qin, "Ms. Qin, *please* allow Angel to continue acting on the television show!"

"But her studies . . ."

"I will help her," said Lily. "I will help her with her schoolwork, I promise. Ms. Qin, please say it's all right with you!"

Ms. Qin agreed.

So, just as before, every day after school Angel's mother took her to the television studio in a taxi. But NOT quite just as before, because now Angel and Lily were friends!

INVITATIONS

Lily's birthday was coming up soon.

Her mother said she could have a small birthday party, and Lily decided she would invite just two or three special friends.

Lily would definitely invite Man Man, because she had been to Man Man's birthday party last week. She was going to ask her new friend, Angel, but she would be at the television studio. Lily really *wanted* to invite Hippo, but she was too shy to do it herself, so she asked Man Man for help.

"You want to invite Hippo?" Man Man was

surprised. "If you're going to invite Hippo, then you should also invite Wen."

Wen had been invited to Man Man's birthday party, but Lily thought he was a very boring boy who always liked to use big words.

She much preferred Hippo because he hardly spoke at all.

After school, Man Man called over to Hippo, who was playing with Mo, Penguin, and Monkey.

"Hippo, come over here! I've got something to ask you."

"What's up?" Hippo yelled.

"I have something to tell you. Come over here."

"What is it?" Hippo yelled back.

"I don't want the others to hear," Man Man said loudly.

"Others," of course, meant Mo, Penguin, and Monkey, and they were furious that Man Man only wanted to talk to Hippo.

"Don't go over there, Hippo. You don't know what she might do to you!"

Hippo hesitated. Should he go over or not?

Then Man Man sent him a note: "COME SOON OR YOU WILL REGRET IT."

How could he refuse? He ran over to Man Man.

"Hippo, Lily wants to invite you to her birthday party. But she doesn't want the others to go, so don't tell them."

Hippo went back to the other boys. They asked him what Man Man had said.

But Hippo kept silent.

"What's up?" said Mo, annoyed. "Come on, Hippo, tell us!"

Hippo still said nothing.

Of the four friends, Monkey was the cleverest so he slyly asked, "Hippo, just tell us whether it's good or bad."

Hippo answered honestly, "It's good."

Penguin was upset. "Well, if it's something good, why won't you tell us?"

Mo got even angrier. "Who are your *real* friends, Hippo? Me, Monkey, and Penguin or Man Man?"

"You are, of course. Man Man is just a *girl*."

"Then you have to tell us," said Mo.

"Okay, okay. Man Man said that Lily wants to invite me to her birthday party . . ."

"Lily wants you to go, but not us?" the others yelled.

Hippo nodded.

Penguin stamped his foot. "That's not fair. If any of us is invited it should be me. I'm her desk-mate."

Monkey reminded him, "Not anymore, you're not. Wen is her desk-mate now."

"But I WAS—before!"

Monkey was also fed up. Usually people invited *him* to their parties, because he could make up funny rhymes and jokes. He made parties fun!

Mo thought that Lily must still be upset about the pictures, or that Man Man had not passed the invitation on to Mo.

So each one decided to ask Lily why she hadn't invited him to her party.

Penguin was first. He was a little bit flustered and thought he might cry.

"Lily . . ." He didn't get any further because he started to cry.

Lily didn't know what had happened. "Penguin, why are you crying?"

"Why didn't you invite me to your party? Sniff, sniff. . . ."

Lily hated seeing anyone cry, so she said, "Don't cry, Penguin! Of course you can come to my party."

Penguin could turn on the tears like water from a faucet. He could also turn them off. Once Lily had said he could go to her party, the tears stopped.

Penguin rushed back to Monkey and said, "Lily just invited me to her party!"

So Monkey went over to talk to Lily.

"Lily, can you imagine your party without me?"

"Um . . . yes," said Lily.

Monkey frowned. "It would be boring," he continued.

"A party without me would be a party without fun.
A party without fun would be oh-so-glum!
Invite me, Lily, invite me please!
Then your party will go like a breeze!"

Lily knew that Monkey would go on and on with his silly rhymes if she didn't invite him, so she gave in.

Then Monkey rushed back to Mo and said, "Lily invited me to her party too!"

Mo decided to talk to Man Man instead of Lily. "Have you told Lily not to invite me?" he asked.

 57

Man Man and Mo got into an argument almost every day. She was used to it so she didn't pay any attention.

Mo continued. "Tell me why Lily invited Hippo, Penguin, and Monkey to her birthday party and not me!"

"It's not *my* birthday party. Why don't you ask Lily?" Man Man snapped back.

"I'm asking you!" said Mo, ignoring Lily, who was standing there.

"Mo, don't be silly," Lily interrupted. "Of course you can come to my birthday party."

Mo was ecstatic. He rushed back to tell Hippo, Penguin, and Monkey. "Lily invited me!"

THE COOLEST PRESENT

Lily only really wanted to invite one boy to her birthday party—and that boy was Hippo. But she ended up asking all four friends: Mo, the mischievous one; Penguin, the greedy one; Monkey, the chatterbox; and Hippo, the quiet one. But she had forgotten someone and there was more trouble to come.

Wen, Lily's new desk-mate, thought that *he* should be invited. It wasn't fair that she had already invited four boys, leaving him out. But Wen always made everything sound complicated.

"Lily, you are not the Lily I know," he said sadly.

"Who is the Lily you know?" asked Lily.

Wen rolled his eyes, stared at the ceiling and replied, "The Lily I know would never invite guys like Mo, Penguin, Monkey, or Hippo to her birthday party. They would make the party a total mess, a complete disaster, a CATASTROPHIC event."

Wen loved to talk like this. He used as many long words as he could. Some people said he had swallowed a dictionary when he was a baby. Lily thought he would never stop, so she interrupted him.

"Then you . . ."

"Please don't interrupt me!" Wen carried on. "Your parents will be shocked by those troublemakers. They will think all the boys in their daughter's class behave like that."

"Then tell me, what kind of boys *should* be invited?"

"Boys like me."

Wen was *not* a modest boy.

Lily knew he would say something like that. She had invited so many boys now that one more wouldn't make any difference.

"All right, then I will invite you!" she said, cranky.

"You could ask me in a little more friendly manner," said Wen.

Lily was getting really fed up. She was starting to regret even having a party. She shouted at Wen, "I've already invited you! What else do you want?"

Wen decided to shut up.

For the next few days, the boys thought about their birthday presents for Lily.

Mo had never given a birthday present to a girl, not even Angel, who was his neighbor. He wanted to give Lily something really special, but he needed to find out what the other boys were going to give her first.

"Penguin, what are you giving Lily for her birthday?"

Penguin was chewing something and didn't want to say much. He just said, "No comment."

Mo pretended to be surprised and replied, "Ah, you mean you have no idea what to give her?"

Penguin immediately replied, "I'm going to give her a souvenir from one of my vacations overseas."

Penguin had visited lots of countries with his father. He often showed off in front of Mo and his classmates about it. But he'd never been generous enough to give any of his souvenirs to them.

 61

Mo then asked Monkey, who said that he had already bought a musical birthday card. But it was too small for everything he wanted to write in it. So he was going to buy an extra-large birthday card to write a special birthday rhyme for Lily.

What nonsense, thought Mo.

Then Mo turned to Hippo.

"Hippo, what are *you* giving Lily for her birthday?"

Hippo always looked like a sleepy dog. He opened his eyes and said, "I have no idea. I probably won't give her anything."

Mo knew that Hippo was the only boy Lily really wanted to invite to her party, and he wasn't even going to give her a present. Hippo had no idea how to treat a girl!

Mo thought long and hard but couldn't think of anything that he might give to Lily that would be really special. Then he had an idea!

Mo called his uncle. He was unmarried and in his thirties. Since he occasionally gave presents to girls, he would know what Mo should give Lily.

Mo said, "Uncle Dink, a girl in my class is having a birthday soon, and she insisted that I come to her birthday party. Can you tell me what present I should give her?"

Uncle Dink was munching an apple. He said, "Give her a melon."

"A melon?"

"Yeah. Flowers are so . . . predictable."

"Oh, right. I bet Wen will give her flowers. And I bet he'll give her ten roses because it's her tenth birthday."

Uncle Dink started to munch his apple again. "Who's Wen?" he asked. "Is he competing with you for this girl?"

Mo hung up the phone.

A MELON FOR LILY

Mo took Uncle Dink's advice and decided to buy a melon for Lily as a birthday present. He thought it was better to give a melon than flowers. Melons could be eaten; there was no way to eat flowers!

Lily's birthday was on Saturday, so they had no school. Mo got up early and went to the supermarket to buy a melon.

There was a large variety of melons in the fruit section: watermelon, cantaloupe, honeydew melon, and others.

Mo chose a honeydew melon. It didn't look quite

as nice as a watermelon, but he liked the sound of the name and it made his mouth water just thinking about it.

The honeydew melon Mo bought was really big—it weighed four kilos—and it felt heavy in his backpack.

Mo carried the melon straight to Lily's apartment.

After Mo had pressed the bell a few times, a man wearing a bathrobe opened the door.

"Excuse me, but my name is Mo, and I've come to celebrate Lily's birthday."

The man blinked, not quite believing what he was seeing. But Mo just barged in through the door.

Lily came out of her room. She was also wearing a bathrobe and her hair was loose. Mo didn't know she had such long hair. Usually she tied it back like a dancer.

Lily didn't seem very happy to see Mo. In fact, she looked annoyed.

"Mo, why are you so early?"

"I wanted to be the first to arrive."

"But my birthday party isn't till this afternoon. I haven't even eaten breakfast!"

"Oh, I don't mind waiting. You go ahead and enjoy your breakfast!" said Mo.

"How can I eat while you're here watching me?" asked Lily.

"Just pretend I'm not here—ignore me, like you do in school," replied Mo.

Lily couldn't believe it. She had so many things to do before her party and she didn't want Mo here, getting in her way. She didn't want to be rude, but she had to do something to get rid of him. So with her sweetest ballerina smile she said, "Mo, would you please go home right now? Come to my party this afternoon, okay?"

"Okay, I'll go. See you later," said Mo.

Mo didn't seem at all bothered. He wouldn't have had much fun at Lily's aparment without his friends being there anyway.

Mo picked up his melon and went home. He didn't want to leave it in Lily's aparment, in case his friends turned up early and saw it. He didn't want anyone to know that the honeydew melon was Mo's gift to Lily. He would go home and carve some words on it.

Mo soon discovered that carving words on a melon was not as easy as he'd thought. Every time he made a cut, some juice came out, so Mo had to keep licking

 67

his fingers. He almost ate a whole piece of melon. It was delicious!

Then the melon kept sliding off the table, so there was juice on the floor, which he had to mop up. But Mo kept carving. Soon he had a very special birthday melon to give to Lily at her party.

After lunch, Mo set out again for Lily's apartment. On the way he noticed Wen just ahead of him, carrying

*The melon says *HAPPY BIRTHDAY, LILY!* in Chinese.

something that looked suspiciously like roses.

Mo caught up with Wen and counted ten roses in Wen's hand.

Mo laughed. "Wen, I guessed it!"

"What did you guess?" Wen asked.

"Your birthday present for Lily. Ten roses, right? I knew that ages ago," replied Mo.

"How could you know what I was going to give Lily before I did?" Wen asked Mo.

"You've been watching corny television shows where men give their girlfriends roses. I think you must LOVE Lily!" Mo teased.

"Well, it's better than your present—are you giving her that stupid melon?" Wen asked.

They argued on the sidewalk, in the elevator, and in front of the door to Lily's apartment. Then Man Man showed up.

"What are you two arguing about? It's Lily's birthday!" Man Man scolded.

Lily came to the door dressed in a lacy white dress, looking like Snow White. Mo thought that Lily in an ordinary dress was beautiful enough. Wearing this dress, she was a princess.

When everyone had arrived at Lily's home, it was

time to give her their presents.

Man Man gave her a cuddly little teddy bear.

Typical girly present, thought Mo.

Penguin gave her a seashell. He kept saying it was a seashell all the way from Hawaii, but Mo knew that you could get those shells anywhere. The shell he'd brought back with him from the beach was exactly the same.

Penguin was desperate to make Lily believe that this was a Hawaiian seashell, so he held the seashell to Lily's ear and explained, "Can you hear it? Can you hear the sound of the waves from Hawaii?"

Lily heard a droning in her ear, as if a dozen bees were fluttering inside.

"I've never been to Hawaii," she said. "How should I know what the waves in Hawaii sound like?"

Mo laughed. Monkey laughed even louder. So Penguin was rude to Monkey when he brought out his birthday card with all the writing on it. Just as Monkey was about to read, Penguin yelled, "Don't bother to listen, Lily. It will just be a bunch of nonsense!"

"How do you know it's nonsense? I haven't even read one word yet," said Monkey.

Monkey was upset. He decided he'd wait for Lily to read his card when she was by herself.

It was time for Wen to give his present. When Man Man saw the ten red roses, she seemed strangely annoyed.

"Wen, your gift isn't exactly original," Man Man said.

"Who said I could only give flowers to you? Why can't I give flowers to Lily?" Wen asked Man Man.

The others giggled. So, when Man Man had celebrated *her* tenth birthday, Wen had given *her* ten roses. Aha!

Hippo had said he wasn't giving Lily a present, so Mo decided to show him up.

"Hippo, give Lily your present, come on!"

But then Hippo took a package out of his pocket. He *had* gotten Lily a present!

PISGES

Hippo gave Lily a pen, which made Mo feel better because it was quite an ordinary present. But Mo didn't realize that it was a special pen.

"Lily, your astrological sign is on the pen," said Hippo. "Look, it's Pisces."

"Wow, what a *special* gift!" Lily exclaimed.

Man Man snatched the pen from Hippo, and read out the words on the pen: "'Pisces—tender and romantic, sympathetic and very generous. Believes in perfectionism, is imaginative, has a calm nature, is sensitive and thoughtful but lacks confidence and stamina.'"

Lily grabbed the pen back from Man Man and held her treasure in her hands. "Thank you, Hippo. It's a *really special* present."

The other boys glared at Hippo. It appeared that he had cheated them all.

Mo couldn't stop himself from blushing. "Hippo, you said you weren't bringing a gift."

"My mother said that I couldn't go to someone else's birthday party without taking a present," replied Hippo. "I saw a box of pens with different star signs on them. I chose the pen with Pisces on it. . . ."

No one had ever heard Hippo say so much at one time! But Wen was much more concerned about something else.

Wen looked at Hippo in amazement. Not even *he* knew Lily's astrological sign.

"Hippo, how did you know Lily's sign?"

Hippo replied, "It's written on the pen that anyone born between February twenty-first and March twentieth is Pisces."

Wen saw the words on the pen. For once he had nothing to say.

But Monkey did. He said the description of Pisces on the pen wasn't at all like Lily.

"Lily doesn't *lack confidence*. How can a person who walks like her *lack confidence*?"

Monkey imitated Lily—walking with his shoulders back, chin held high, and eyes looking straight ahead.

"You're right," said Penguin. He was jealous of Hippo because Lily was not as interested in his present. So he decided to criticize Hippo's gift too. "Would someone who *lacks stamina* be able to be a ballerina like Lily? This pen is stupid!"

Wen clapped. So did Monkey.

"What are you doing? Stop bullying him!" said Man Man. She felt sorry for Hippo. "Hippo, I'm an Aquarius, but you didn't give me a birthday present!"

Hippo said, "You didn't invite me to your birthday party. How could I give you a gift?"

"Huh!" Man Man snorted.

Penguin no longer cared about Hippo's gift. He just wanted to eat birthday cake.

"Attention!" Mo shouted at the top of his voice. "I haven't given Lily *my* gift!"

Penguin was impatient. "Hurry up then, Mo."

Mo held out the honeydew melon.

The other boys fell down laughing.

"Mo, what *is* that?"

Mo pointed at what he had carved on the melon skin: HAPPY BIRTHDAY, LILY!

*The melon says *HAPPY BIRTHDAY, LILY!* in Chinese.

"That's STUPID," said Wen. "I've never seen anyone give a *melon* as a birthday present."

"Melon is SO now," Mo began. "It's SO uncool to

send flowers. It's cool to give a melon. That's what my uncle told me."

Everybody knew that Mo's uncle was cool. He knew all the latest trends, so they believed him.

Lily's birthday cake was a double layer chocolate one that was big enough for everyone to have a piece. But the cake was very sweet and they all felt a little sick from eating so much. Lily's mother's plan was that after eating the cake they would all watch Lily perform some ballet. But everyone was too full and too sleepy to do anything.

"Attention." Again, Mo shouted at the top of his voice. "We haven't eaten the honeydew melon!"

"Mo, we can't do that!" said Man Man. "The honeydew melon was a gift for Lily."

"But *I* gave it to her!" Mo replied. "It will be meaningless if it's not eaten at the birthday party."

Man Man thought about it. "Maybe eating honeydew melon at a birthday party would be wishing Lily sweetness like honeydew melon every day."

So Lily's mother brought out the cut honeydew melon. The pieces were golden yellow and very beautiful.

Penguin took a piece of honeydew melon and said, "*I* think eating honeydew melon at a birthday party will refresh the mouth after the sweetness of chocolate cake."

So Mo knew that *his* gift of a honeydew melon was the coolest present of all!

A CAT'S TALE

When Lily found an injured cat by the road, she held it in her arms and took it home to look after. Lily loved the cat, who she named Babe. At first she fed it milk from an eyedropper. Then her father bought, cooked, and cut up pork liver and a little fish every day and mixed them with the milk to feed Babe. But now Lily's father was going to America as a visiting scholar for six months. Lily's mother went out early and got back home late from work. She barely had time to prepare meals for the family, so there would be no time to look after a cat.

Lily's mother wanted to give Babe away. She had asked lots of people to take her, but they all gave excuses because the cat was so ordinary. Finally, she found someone who wanted a cat to catch the large number of mice in his house. Babe would be taken away tomorrow.

Lily was very unhappy. She didn't want her cat to be given away. She thought if Babe were adopted by a classmate, she would be able to get her back when her father returned from America.

The first classmate Lily asked for help was Hippo.

"Hippo, will you look after my cat, Babe, for me, please?" asked Lily.

Hippo always wanted to please Lily, but he couldn't help her. "I'm sorry," he said. "If it were a dog I would help you."

"Why not a cat?" asked Lily.

"Lily, do you know which animal I'm most scared of?"

"A tiger? Or maybe a crocodile?" asked Lily.

"Neither. It's a cat. When I was a baby, I was badly scratched by a cat. Here, look. On the back of my hand, there are three scars left from when the cat scratched me. Since then I've always been terrified of cats."

Lily could not leave her most beloved cat in the care of someone who would be afraid of it.

The second classmate Lily asked was Penguin. She knew Penguin liked food, so he would feed Babe well.

Penguin said that he already had a cat at home. His cat was very rare—a Persian cat with one blue eye and one yellow eye. He asked Lily, "Is your cat a Persian one?"

"No, she's just a stray I found on the street," said Lily. "Will you look after her for me, please?"

"Sorry, Lily, I can't look after such an *ordinary* cat, because my pedigreed cat would fight with it."

The third classmate Lily asked was Wen.

"Wen, I need your help," said Lily.

"Good," said Wen. "I am very good at giving help."

"Will you look after my cat for a little while?" asked Lily.

Wen looked nervous. "How long would you like me to look after it?"

 81

"Six months," said Lily. "That's how long my father will be abroad. I'll take her back when he returns."

"That's too long," said Wen. "But two or three days would be all right."

Lily didn't think she was going to find anyone to look after Babe. When she thought about her cat being taken away tomorrow and that she would never see her cat again, Lily started to cry.

"Lily's crying!"

"Lily's crying!"

Other girls cried in class, but Lily hardly ever did. Everyone was wondering why she was crying.

Everyone except for Hippo, Penguin, and Wen.

They knew *exactly* why she was crying.

Hippo hated himself for being scared of cats. If Lily had asked him to feed a dog, a tiger, or even a crocodile for her, he would have done it. He needed to find someone who wasn't scared of cats to look after Lily's cat.

Hippo asked Mo whether he was scared of cats.

"Why *should* I be scared of cats?" said Mo. "I'm not a mouse."

Hippo knew he was like a mouse when it came to cats. But he didn't dare tell Mo he was scared of them, because he was scared Mo would call him a mouse in front of his classmates.

Hippo told Mo why Lily was crying. Mo rushed over to Lily.

"Lily, I'm upset. Do you know why?" he asked. "Why didn't you ask *me* to look after your cat? I would be happy to do it."

"You?"

Lily hadn't wanted to ask Mo to look after Babe, because she thought he was too mischievous to look after her properly.

Lily used Hippo's excuse. "But you're scared of cats," she said.

"No, I'm not," said Mo.

Then Lily used Penguin's excuse. "My cat is not a rare Persian breed. She's just an ordinary one I rescued from the street."

"An ordinary cat is still a cat," said Mo.

Lily used Wen's excuse. "You would need to look after her for six whole months, not just for two or three days."

"That's fine," said Mo. "No problem."

Lily had no idea how to refuse him. She said that someone was coming to take the cat away from her house tomorrow, so Mo would need to begin his cat-sitting duties the very next day.

"I will come home with you after school tomorrow and take the cat away," he said.

How could Lily refuse Mo's offer?

PARTNERS

"Don't forget I'm going home with you after school," Mo said to Lily when classes were over.

Wen, Lily's desk-mate, was curious.

"Why are you going to Lily's house, Mo?" he asked.

"I'm not telling you!" Mo replied.

"Let *me* tell you," said Lily. "He's coming to get my cat because he is going to look after her for six months."

That shut Wen up.

When school was over, Mo walked with Lily instead of Hippo, Penguin, and Monkey.

"Where are you going?" asked Penguin.

"I'm going to Lily's house," said Mo.

"If you're going, we're going too," replied Penguin.

"He's coming to get my cat," Lily explained.

That shut Penguin and Hippo up.

Now, only Monkey wanted to go with them.

When they got to Lily's aparment, Lily unlocked the door and her mother was there.

"You're home already, Mom."

"The man is coming for the cat. I just came back to get it ready."

Lily gasped. Mo stared.

"Lily said the man was coming *tomorrow*," said Mo.

"Well," said Lily's mom. "Now he's coming today."

Lily pulled Mo into her room. "That man will be here soon," she said. "What can we do now?"

Mo said to Monkey, "Go and keep Lily's mother talking, Monkey. Make up some story, just keep her out of the way . . . whatever."

"Why?" said Lily. "What good will that do?"

"I want him to distract her," Mo told her.

Monkey loved to talk, especially in rhyme. He'd soon made something up to keep Lily's mom away from her daughter and Mo.

"Hi, I'm Monkey, Lily's friend from school.
I can't do ballet, but I am real cool.
You look like a mom who's more like a sister,
Have you got a Band-Aid for my blister?"

Lily's mom laughed. She liked to think she looked young. But the boy said he had a blister, so she had better help him.

"Where's your blister, young man? Let me see," she said.

"Oh no," said Monkey. "It's on my foot and I can't take my shoes and socks off in front of you."

"Okay, I understand. Even my husband's feet get a little smelly at the end of the day. I'll get you a Band-Aid," said Lily's mom.

While her mother was looking for a Band-Aid, Lily grabbed the cat from the hallway and took it to her room.

Lily's mom gave Monkey the Band-Aid and then said, "Where did the other boy go?"

She stood up and was about to go into Lily's room.

Monkey had to distract her. He thought quickly and said, "That's Mo, a popular guy in our class. He came to Lily's birthday party, remember? He was the one who gave her a honeydew melon. Doesn't Lily ever talk about him?"

"No, she doesn't," Lily's mom said.

Lily seldom spoke of anyone from school. She sometimes mentioned the girls but never the boys. So Monkey could make up a story about Mo.

"He's the worst student in class, while Lily is the best. The best should help the worst. Don't you agree?" asked Monkey.

Lily's mom agreed as she walked to the door.

Monkey sat there, facing the door to Lily's room. Mo opened the door slightly. He blinked his eyes. Monkey understood that he needed to distract Lily's mom again.

"Ow! Ow!" he yelled suddenly. "My foot really hurts."

Lily's mother was the kind of woman who hated to see anyone in pain. She said she would get some ointment from the bathroom for Monkey's blister.

When her mother was in the bathroom, Lily quickly got some duct tape and a plastic basket from the kitchen. Since she was an excellent ballet dancer, she made no noise when she moved.

Just as she came back from the bathroom, Lily's mother saw Mo coming out of Lily's room.

"Has my daughter helped you enough?" she asked.

"Yes." Mo bowed to her and said politely, "Good-bye, Lily's mom!"

"If you were doing schoolwork, it didn't take long," she said.

Monkey was worried that Lily's mom might realize something was up, so he said, "Just let him go. I am sure Lily is bored with helping such a stupid boy."

"Why don't you go as well?" Lily's mom was

beginning to suspect that something was going on.

"My foot is still sore. Could I just wait here for a few minutes longer?" asked Monkey.

Just at that very moment, the doorbell rang. Lily's mom opened the door and a man walked inside.

Monkey was beginning to panic, but then Lily opened her bedroom door and gave a thumbs-up signal. Now Monkey knew what must have happened. Lily had put the cat in the plastic basket and attached the duct tape to it. She'd lowered the basket down from the window to Mo, who was waiting outside the apartment. Mo must have the cat! What good partners they were—partners-in-catnapping!

RUMORS

Now that Mo was looking after Lily's cat, the two kids could often be seen talking to each other. In the past, Lily never used to talk to Mo, but now they spoke nearly every day.

"Mo, this is Babe's ball. Could you take it home with you, please?"

"But that's an old ball, Lily. Can't I get her a new one?" he said. Mo felt silly saying Babe's name.

"But Babe likes *this* ball," said Lily.

Mo took the ball from Lily. One of the other children saw this and told someone else. A rumor began to spread, and it changed from "Lily gave Mo a ball" to "Lily gave Mo a present."

"Another present?" someone asked. "I saw Lily give Mo a package yesterday."

"Really?"

"Why is Lily giving Mo presents every day?"

"There must be something going on."

Actually, there had been a bag of pork liver in the package. Lily gave Mo food for her cat every two or three days.

Everyone was talking about Mo and Lily. Soon Hippo, Penguin, and Monkey heard the rumor. Monkey knew what it was all about. "Oh, the presents aren't for him. They're for her cat," he said.

Even though they knew what it was all about, Hippo and Penguin were still jealous. Hippo thought that he could have had the cat if only he hadn't been afraid of cats. And Penguin thought if the cat had been a more special one, he could have been the one to look after it.

What they were most jealous of was that Lily and Mo went to the supermarket together after school to buy cat food on days she didn't go to ballet class.

If Lily and Mo went to the supermarket, Penguin,

Hippo, and Monkey went too.

Mo asked them to stop following him and Lily.

"You don't own the supermarket," they said. "If you can go there, why can't we?"

Monkey liked to change sides all the time. Sometimes he sided with Mo. Sometimes, he was on Penguin's side.

"What are you afraid of, Mo? Are you afraid that we may see you two . . . ?" asked Monkey.

He didn't finish his remark. They knew what he was about to say.

Hippo interrupted. "Are you going to marry her when you grow up?"

"Hah!" Penguin fell over laughing. The thought of Lily marrying Mo was hilarious.

It was Hippo who first started the rumor that Mo wanted to marry Lily when he was grown up. But the rumor kept changing. By the time Ms. Qin heard it, it had turned into "Mo wants to marry Lily NOW."

Ms. Qin called Man Man to her office. Since Man Man was supposed to be keeping an eye on Mo and was one of Lily's good friends, Man Man would tell Ms. Qin what was going on.

"Man Man, what is happening between Mo and Lily?" asked Ms. Qin.

"They are always together now," Man Man said. "And Lily often sends him presents. They also go to the supermarket together."

Ms. Qin knew how much Mo had wanted to sit with Lily at the beginning of the semester and that she had had to separate the two. There must be something going on. That was serious. She must have a talk with Lily.

Lily stood in front of Ms. Qin with her chin up and her head high, just as if she were standing on the stage.

"What do you think of Mo, Lily?" asked Ms. Qin.

"He's okay," said Lily.

"Do you mean okay good or okay so-so?" asked Ms. Qin.

"Well, he's caring, loves animals, is honest, and sticks to his word," said Lily.

Ms. Qin wasn't sure if she had found anything out, since she already knew that Mo was all those things.

"Lily, I hear that you two are often together now,

and you go shopping together at the supermarket," said Ms. Qin.

Ms. Qin sounded very serious. Lily wanted to tell the truth, but she didn't want to say any more in case she got Mo into trouble. Ms. Qin might say that Mo should be concentrating on his schoolwork and not on looking after Lily's cat.

Ms. Qin continued. "As a good student in school, you must behave yourself outside school. Now run along and don't get involved in any of Mo's mischief."

As soon as she left Ms. Qin's office, Lily went to the supermarket with Mo. They had planned to buy some food for Babe today.

They continued in this manner all the time that Mo was looking after Lily's cat. Soon the rumor vanished and Ms. Qin left them alone. Hippo, Penguin, and Monkey weren't jealous of them anymore. Lily and Mo were just good friends. But the four boys were more than that—they were the BEST of friends!

READERS' NOTE

MO'S WORLD

Mo Shen Ma lives in a big city in China. Modern Chinese cities are very much like ours, so his life is not so different from your own: he goes to school, watches television, and gets into mischief—just like kids all over the world!

There are *some* differences, though. Chinese writing is completely unlike our own. There is no alphabet, and words are not made up of letters—instead, each word is represented by a little drawing called a *character*. For us, learning to read is easy. There are only twenty-six letters that make up all our words! But in Chinese, every word has its own character. Even Simplified Chinese writing uses a basis of 6,800 different characters. Each character has to be learned by heart, which means that it takes many years for a Chinese student to learn to read fluently.

NAMES

Chinese personal names carry various meanings, and the names in this book have definitely been chosen for a reason! Take Mo Shen, the hero of our tale. His name is made up of the words *Mo*, which means "good ideas," and *Shen*, which means "deep" or "profound." So you can see how much his name suits him, because Mo Shen is always coming up with great ideas!

There are some names that are very common in China. For example, the most popular girl in Mo's class also has a very popular name—Lily. Her name means "purity" and "beauty." It's the perfect name for the most beautiful girl in class!

Mo's archrival is Man Man. Her name means "really slow." In China, there is a tradition of giving children names that are the exact opposite of their real character. Man Man always wants to know what's going on. No one would ever accuse Man Man of being slow!

STORY BACKGROUND

In this story, Mo and his friends celebrate Children's Day. This event takes place every year on June 1 for kids all over China. On this day children receive cards and presents, eat special foods, and sometimes they even have parades.

Even though children still have to go to school on their special day, they don't have to attend class and they don't have to worry about doing homework! Many elementary schools like Mo's celebrate with performances by students, much like what Lily does when she dances ballet for the school.

Parents sometimes take their children to visit interesting sites to help them learn more about Chinese history and culture, such as museums or the Great Wall. And best of all, on Children's Day, places such as movie theaters, parks, and children's museums offer free admission.

Enjoy more of Mo's Mischief
with this sneak peek at

SUPER COOL UNCLE

A BRAND-NEW HUMAN

Mo's mother had a brother and his name was Dink. Mo thought his uncle was the coolest person he had ever met. Uncle Dink had gone to college in Shanghai and then moved on to Beijing, where he was a whiz kid with computers. He'd then moved to different cities in China for work, but now he was coming home.

Mo hadn't seen his uncle for years, but he'd heard his parents and their friends calling Uncle Dink a "brand-new human."

"Dad, what's the difference between brand-new humans and humans like us?"

Mo and his father, Mr. Ma, were on their way to the airport to meet Uncle Dink.

"Brand-new humans are very different from us, Mo. They work hard, but they also play hard; they don't mind what people think about them and they like to be noticed. When you see Uncle Dink, you'll know what I mean!"

To Mo, Uncle Dink was as mysterious as the abominable snowman and he couldn't wait to see him.

"What does Uncle Dink do?" Mo asked.

"He's a computer software engineer. A very clever businessman who will make lots of money."

Mo immediately formed a picture of Uncle Dink in his mind: a fancy haircut, polished black shoes, a stylish single-breasted jacket with two buttons or an equally fashionable double-breasted jacket with four buttons, a pure-silk tie that was heavy and thick, and a big, shiny briefcase.

When they got to the airport, they saw on the arrival board that Uncle Dink's flight had arrived.

Many savvy businessmen and businesswomen walked into the terminal, dragging their suitcases behind them, but there was no sign of Uncle Dink.

"Do you think we have the right flight?" Mo asked anxiously.

"I think so," said Mr. Ma, taking out a small piece of paper from his jacket pocket: "Flight 4107. That's right."

Mo had made a card with *Welcome Home, Uncle Dink* written on it. Mo's handwriting was very sloppy, especially when using big felt markers, but he had managed to write the words nice and big.

Mo held the card up high—he was afraid that Uncle Dink would sneak away and get a taxi.

Then a young man with rainbow-colored hair, tight leather pants, and a leather jacket covered in studs and zippers walked straight toward Mo. He stopped in front of the board, craned his neck to one side, and tried very hard not to laugh.

"Hi, Dink!" Even Mr. Ma had great difficulty in recognizing his wife's brother.

"Brother-in-law!" said the man. Then he pointed at

Mo. "Is this little Mo, your precious only son?"

"Who else could he be?" said Mr. Ma. He looked around. "Where's your luggage?"

"This is it."

Mo could see that Uncle Dink was only carrying a laptop in one hand and a cell phone in the other. Uncle Dink said, "I have a laptop, a cell phone, a credit card, and a passport. It's enough for me to travel around the world and live a happy life."

Uncle Dink held Mo's hand and headed off toward the parking garage. He had such long legs that Mo practically had to run to keep up with him.

Mr. Ma drove Uncle Dink to his parents' house. During the ride, Mo couldn't stop staring at Uncle Dink. He looked more like a pop star than a businessman!

Like Mr. Ma, Grandpa and Grandma had not seen Uncle Dink for two or three years. His colorful hair alone was enough to make them almost faint.

"Oh no, Dink," said Grandma. "Someone has dropped paint on your head!"

Mo's grandma tried to persuade Uncle Dink to wash the paint out of his hair. Uncle Dink found it both funny and annoying.

"Don't be silly!" said Mo. "That's not paint. Uncle Dink *wanted* to have his hair dyed like that."

Grandpa and Grandma remained confused. "Why would he do that?"

Mr. Ma, worrying about more quarreling, suggested that Dink might be tired from his flight and want to relax in his room.

"Oh, I'm not staying here," Uncle Dink explained. "The company has rented an apartment for me."

"Ridiculous!" said Grandpa. "We have plenty of rooms, but you would rather stay in a rented apartment. It doesn't make sense."

Grandma was upset too. "You spoiled son. We have kept everything the same in your room, even though you have been away for years. Your room is just as it was, and your guitar and your tennis racket are still in the same place. Nothing has been changed."

Grandma got angrier as she spoke, and Uncle Dink felt guilty. He put his arm around his mother to comfort her.

Mo realized that Grandpa and Grandma still had no idea that Uncle Dink had become a brand-new human. That was why they couldn't understand his weird behavior. But Mo could. How could someone be a brand-new human if he hadn't changed at all?

"Grandpa and Grandma, I'm afraid there is one thing you still don't know—Uncle Dink has become a brand-new human!"

"What's a brand-new human? An alien?" Grandma asked. "I gave birth to this boy—how could he turn into an alien?"

Grandma grabbed Uncle Dink's arm. "Did you get abducted by aliens and were forced to become an alien too?"

Grandma had seen something about UFOs in the newspapers and on TV. *She is very old, but she has a*

good imagination, thought Mo.

Uncle Dink gave up. He knew he would never be able to persuade his parents that he was a modern man and that he didn't live in the dark ages like they did. Mr. Ma drove him to an apartment building in the city where he would be living. The apartment was on the twenty-ninth floor and Mo was desperate to see it, but his dad wanted to get home.

When he said good-bye, Uncle Dink gave Mo an unexpected smile. Mo thought this was a good sign. Uncle Dink liked him!